Saying Good-bye to Grandma

Saying Good-bye to Grandma

by JANE RESH THOMAS

illustrated by Marcia Sewall

CLARION BOOKS

New York

Clarion Books
a Houghton Mifflin Company imprint
215 Park Avenue South, New York, NY 10003
Text copyright © 1988 by Jane Resh Thomas
Illustrations copyright © 1988 by Marcia Sewall

Library of Congress Cataloging-in-Publication Data
Thomas, Jane Resh.
Saying good-bye to grandma.

Summary: Seven-year-old Suzie is curious and fearful
about what Grandma's funeral will be like.
[1. Funeral rites and ceremonies—Fiction. 2. Death—
Fiction. 3. Grandmothers—Fiction] I. Sewall, Marcia.
ill. II. Title.
PZ7.T36695Say 1988   [E]   87-20826
ISBN 0-89919-645-4   PA ISBN 0-395-54779-2

BP 10 9 8 7 6 5 4 3

For my family, in memory of Mary Corbett Resh

I

The day that Grandma died, we drove all afternoon and half the night going back to the place where Mom and Dad grew up.

I sat in the back and wondered what happens at a funeral, while Mom told stories about Grandma in the dark. "Remember, Suzie, the time Grandma trapped a raccoon in the garbage can?" Mom asked, wiping her eyes. "No, that would have been five or six years ago, when you were a baby."

Mom looked out the window for a minute before she talked again. "Grandma said, 'That coon
dumps the garbage faster than I can clean it up.'
But she let him go when she saw his little face
peeking out through a crack underneath the lid. 'If
you can't beat 'em, join 'em,' Grandma said. So
she bought a garbage can with a latch. And she
served the rascal a special plate of table scraps
every night."

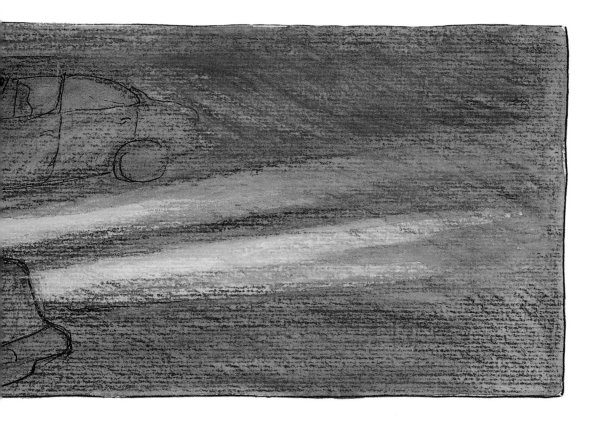

Mom blew her nose and turned in her seat to look at me. "Remember the apple pies lined up on the cupboard? And the jars of peaches Grandma canned in the hottest days of August?"

"I remember when Grandma taught me to embroider," I said. "She never minded if I didn't sew straight lines."

I fell asleep hungry, thinking about Grandma's apple pies.

When I woke up, I was in bed between my dad and mom. I picked Dad's eyes open with my fingers, but they were white inside. He was still asleep.

The bathroom in the motel was fancier than ours at home, with gold faucets on the sink and eight white towels folded in a stack. For breakfast, Dad and I had pancakes and eggs and orange juice. Mom couldn't eat her French toast, so we ate that, too.

We drove all day again before we got to Grandpa's house. Everybody met us in the yard. Mom and Grandpa hugged and cried. Aunt Judy hugged me, and her face was wet.

"Look how much you've grown since last time," said Uncle Dick, measuring me against his side. But the cousins were still all bigger than me. When they ran off to play, I went in the house with Mom and Dad.

Mom put on her jeans and helped Aunt Betty
and Aunt Judy cook the chicken, laughing because
they were in each other's way. Uncle Jim and I set
the table. I looked around the corner for Grandma
in her flowered apron, even though I knew she
wasn't there.

The grownups picked at their food at supper-
time. Grandpa took just one bite of bread; then he

folded his napkin and put it on his plate. The kids
ate all the drumsticks, but none of us talked very
much.

After supper, we went outside for a game of kick
the can. My cousins were calling, "Olly olly oxen
freeeeeedommmm!" in the evening stillness. Their
cries echoed across the lake. "——Reeedomm!
——Eedom!"

I saw Grandpa standing at the end of the dock, with one hand on a post and the other in his pocket. I stood beside him, and he took my hand. We didn't say a word until the sun had finished going down.

"Grandma liked to watch the sun set," said Grandpa. "She used to sit in that chair there and cast for bass in the evening. She could catch 'em, all right. And she could cook 'em so they'd melt on your tongue before you had a chance to chew."

He handed me Grandma's spinning rod that she had left leaning against her chair, beside Grandpa's own, the last time she fished. A small shiny lure was hooked in one of the eyelets. We cast 'til the light was gone. Grandpa's lure would make a little plop far away from shore. Mine always splashed right near the dock.

"It's in the wrist," said Grandpa. Neither of us had a bite.

That night, my cousin Nathan and I slept foot
to foot on the couch. Jason and Matthew and
Brent and Rachel lined up their sleeping bags and
pillows on the living room floor. They were whispering, but Nathan and I were too tired to whisper
back.

When I woke up, the moon was shining so
bright on the water that I could see everything in
the room. Rachel's eyes were open, too. We lis-

tened to the water lapping on the sand and slap-
ping against the back of the boat. A bird or
something I never heard before was chucking in
the yard. And in the next room, in Grandma and
Grandpa's bedroom, somebody was crying.

Rachel opened up her sleeping bag and made
a place for me. She put her arm around my
shoulder. We lay awake together for a long time,
listening to Grandpa cry.

II

We went swimming in the morning before the grownups woke. Dad rushed out, barefoot in pajamas, and hollered. "Everybody out of the water 'til the lifeguard hunts up a swimsuit!"

We waited on the dock, shivering. The door slammed shut, and Dad ran right into the water with his pajama pants on. "I couldn't find a suit," he said when he came up for air.

Mom fussed around Grandpa at the breakfast table, offering him food. "Have some eggs and bacon, Daddy, or at least a glass of milk." I never heard her call him that before.

Grandpa fussed over his grown-up children, Mom and Uncle Dick and my Aunt Betty. "Have some berries or some toast," he said. "You'll find some cereal in the cupboard there, my boy."

The kids were all so hungry from swimming that we ate everything left over.

We played on the beach all day, so Rachel's hair and mine was still damp when we drove into town to say good-bye to Grandma. I didn't want to go. I was afraid she'd be so changed I wouldn't know her.

"I forgot what Grandma looks like," I told my mom.

She showed me the snapshot she carries in her wallet, the one of Grandma holding up that five-pound fish she caught once. "It's hard to remember, isn't it," said Mom, "when we live so far away."

I squeezed hands with Mom and Dad when we went inside the funeral home. It smelled like Mom's closet the time she dropped her perfume, or like a flower shop. The place looked something like a house, with chairs and couches against every wall.

Grandma was lying in a big brown coffin at the end of a long room with flowers all around. The cover was lifted back. Everybody waited while Grandpa stood alone, with his hand on Grandma's. I went up and took his other hand. Mom and Dad came closer, too.

"That was her favorite dress," said Grandpa. He wiped his eyes with his handkerchief. "I remember when she made it." She was wearing the pink dress she sewed last summer when I stayed with her.

I tried not to look at her face, but I couldn't help it. There was powder on her cheeks, more than she usually wore, and her eyes were shut. She looked the same as always, like she was sleeping on a big soft satin pillow.

"Can I touch her?" I asked Grandpa. He nodded, and I touched Grandma's hand, wishing I could wake her up. I wished that she would turn and smile and hold me the way she used to do. Her hand was cold.

After a while, friends came to visit with my family and say good-bye to Grandma. Her next-door neighbor Allie was there, dressed up in her Sunday clothes, with ruffles on her collar, and a big black purse. Grandpa's friend Virgil stayed at Grandpa's side; he hardly talked at all, but he stayed close.

A woman with red hair squinted her eyes and asked my mom, "Are you Will's sister?"

"This young thing my sister?" said Grandpa, putting his arm around Mom's waist. "Your eyes must be going bad, Mabel. You remember our beautiful youngest daughter Ann."

Everybody talked in quiet voices. There was nothing much for kids to do. I looked around and saw that Brent and Nathan and Matthew were gone. Jason and Rachel had disappeared, too, so I went looking for them.

In a dark room at the bottom of the stairs, I heard whispering. I opened the door a little bit and saw Rachel in the light from the hall, crouched behind a casket like the one that Grandma lay in.

"Don't be scared," Rachel whispered, as she pulled me into the room and closed the door, leaving only a long skinny crack of light. "They're all empty. We checked."

Matthew switched on the light. "We're playing capture the flag with my shoe," he said. All around the room were other empty caskets, some copper-colored, some small and white, all of them high on carts with wheels.

"I'm it," whispered Brent. "You have to sneak up and take the shoe without me catching you." He put it in the middle of the floor and turned off the light.

"I'm going to hide inside a coffin," Jason whispered.

"If you do," said Rachel, "I'll shut the lid."

We played for a long time before the door opened and Mom looked inside. "Suzie," she said to me. I didn't answer. Nobody did. "I know you're in there," she said. "I heard you whispering."

Mom switched on the light and looked around at all the coffins and all the cousins in their hiding places. I thought that she would scold us. But she smiled and put her arm around my shoulder and kissed Nathan on the cheek.

"I'm glad you found a quiet way to let off steam," she said. "The visiting is over now. It's time to go back to Grandma's house and rest."

In the morning, everybody woke up early and dressed in good clothes for the funeral. I went in Grandma's closet and put my face among the dresses that smelled of her cologne. I cried and cried. I could hear my family talking, but I was so quiet nobody missed me until it was time to leave. I heard them all go out. Doors slammed, and cars drove away. I thought they had forgotten all about me.

Then Dad and Mom came back to the house. I heard them call my name. "Suzie! Suzie!"

I didn't answer, but Dad found me anyway. He sat on the floor and held me in his arms, and his voice was husky when he talked. "You don't want to go, I guess."

"If we don't have the funeral," I said, "maybe Grandma will come back home."

"We all want that to be true," said Dad. "But Grandma's gone. Nothing we do can change that. Mom and I are going to her funeral, but you don't have to go. Tanya Baxter said that you can help her at her store."

Mom held me all the way to town.

"What will it be like?" I asked.

"There will be music," Mom said, "and prayers, and friends. And we'll all go with the casket to the cemetery."

I could hear her heart beating in her chest and felt glad she was alive. I decided to go to the funeral with Mom and Dad.

Grandma's casket was already in the front of the church when we went in. The cover was shut. Allie was playing hymns on the organ. Grandpa made room for us beside him, near the end of the bench.

The minister talked for a long time. "Mary brought food and washed our clothes when our son was ill," he said. "Everybody here remembers Mary's kindness." He pointed at the orange and yellow flowers on the altar. "These day lilies came from Mary's garden. She brought bouquets every

Sunday morning all summer long. If she could have done it, she would have gathered the flowers for her own funeral. Mary always liked to help."

I looked around and saw that everybody was crying, even the people who weren't making any noise. It's a good thing Mom brought extra hankies.

We all stood up to sing "Amazing Grace, How Sweet the Sound," Grandma's favorite hymn. Then we waited, hushed, while men in dark suits put the casket in a big car and drove it down the street.

At the cemetery, we all stood on the grass holding on to each other while the minister said more prayers. I looked around at all the bowed heads. Tears streamed down Grandpa's face. Grandpa, who never ever cried, was crying every day. I was afraid that he would fall, but Uncle Dick and Virgil each put an arm around his back. I wished the birds would stop singing for a while.

All of the cousins were quiet there in the cemetery, even Jason and Rachel. The minister gave
everybody a pink rose from the flowers on
Grandma's casket. We left her there in the sun on
the side of the hill, under tall oak trees. As we
walked to the cars, I kept looking back, wonder-
ing who would lower the casket into the ground.
I didn't want to leave my grandma there.

III

We drove back to the church for dinner. Grandma's friends had covered a long white table in the basement with plates of food.

"Help yourself, honey," said Allie, handing me a stiff paper plate.

I was first in line. The ladies had made the table beautiful, with flowers and pretty dishes and all the food arranged just right. Allie followed along, offering me food. There was more than I could eat. Ham, and big rolls to put it on, and relish and

mayonnaise and sliced tomatoes and lettuce and
mustard. Macaroni and cheese, and scalloped
potatoes, and three kinds of Jell-O salad with
whipped cream on top. Potato salad and coleslaw
and carrot sticks.

There was coffee for the grownups, and milk
for the kids. And for dessert, brownies, cherry and
apple pies, and angel food cake with strawberry
topping. My plate was so full it bent.

People in the crowd were laughing now.
Grandpa shook his head when Uncle Dick offered
him a sandwich, but he sipped a cup of tea. Jason
and Brent dodged behind the table and begged
Allie for a sandwich, so they wouldn't starve to
death waiting in line. "Growing boys need special
service," she said, and gave them two sandwiches
apiece. They ate in gulps and then played tag at the
edge of the meeting room.

"Let's go fishing in a couple of days, Will," said Virgil. "Maybe we could go in your boat. I always like to watch the best fisherman on the lake work his magic."

Grandpa smiled. "That sounds good. My family here are only staying through tomorrow."

"We'd like you to come for dinner, Will, after church on Sunday," Mrs. Dale said.

"Why, thank you, Ethel," said Grandpa. "I'll bring a jar of Mary's peaches."

Mom thanked the ladies for feeding us. They were packing up the leftovers so we could take them home with us. "We loved doing one last thing for Mary," Allie said. "Goodness knows, she did so much for us."

Aunt Judy and Uncle Dick's family left the next morning. I waved good-bye to Nathan, Matthew, and Brent. Nathan stuck out his tongue, but then he waved, too. In the afternoon, Aunt Betty and Uncle Jim's family went back home. I kissed Rachel good-bye. Jason said he didn't hug girls, but he hugged me anyway. We stayed another night so Grandpa wouldn't be alone in the house.

In the morning, before we left, Grandpa made the breakfast—scrambled eggs and sausage. This time he ate, too. He thanked me for fishing with him. "We had a good time, didn't we, watching the sun go down?" He hugged me and held my face in his hands. "You helped me make it through the week," he said. "Are you coming for a visit again this summer?"

Mom said maybe I could come on the train in August. Then Grandpa could drive me back and stay awhile with us.

We traveled all day and half the night and half the day again to get back home. Everybody was quiet that first morning in the car.

I watched the cornfields rushing by my window and wondered whether I had been sad enough.

"I thought people didn't do anything but cry for weeks when somebody died," I said after a long while. "But I had fun sometimes at Grandma's funeral."

"I had a good time, too," said Mom. "That's one of the things that funerals are for. We said good-bye to Grandma, and we said hello to our family and friends."

"Grandma would have enjoyed it more than anyone," said Dad. "She loved to gather everybody 'round and cook a feast."

We talked about the dinners Grandma used to cook. I thought about her sitting on the dock to watch the sun go down, and cooking the bass she'd caught so they'd melt on your tongue before you had a chance to chew.

Then I fell asleep and dreamed about taking the train to visit Grandpa in a month. We would talk about Grandma and remember the way things used to be. He would teach me fishing, and we would learn together how to cook.